S0-BFD-242

Fox River Valley PLD
555 Barrington Ave., Dundee, IL 60118
www.frvpld.info
Renew online or call 847-590-8706

Ricky Ricotta's Mighty Robot vs. the Mutant Mosquitoes from Mercury

Ricky Ricotta's Mighty Robot vs. the Mutant Mosquitoes from Mercury

The Second Robot Adventure Novel by
DAV PILKEY

Pictures by
MARTIN ONTIVEROS

Originally published as RICKY RICOTTA'S GIANT ROBOT VS. THE MUTANT MOSQUITOES FROM MERCURY

SCHOLASTIC INC.
New York Toronto London Auckland Sydney
Mexico City New Delhi Hong Kong Buenos Aires

This book is being published simultaneously
in hardcover by the Blue Sky Press.

ISBN-13: 978-0-590-30722-2
ISBN-10: 0-590-30722-3

42 41   12 13/0

Printed in the United States of America   40

First Scholastic paperback printing, September 2000

For Robbie Staenberg — D. P.

To Micki, Derek, Bwana, Marny,
Alicia, Craig, Kalah, JP,
and my cats — M. O.

Chapters

CHAPTER 1

Ricky and His Robot

There once was a mouse named
Ricky Ricotta who lived in
Squeakyville with his mother
and father.

Ricky Ricotta might have been
the smallest mouse around . . .

. . . but he had the BIGGEST
best friend in town.

CHAPTER 2

School Days

Ricky and his Mighty Robot
liked to go to school together.

Sometimes when Ricky
was running late, his Robot
would fly him straight to
the front door.

After school, the Mighty Robot liked to help Ricky with his homework. The Robot's computer brain could solve complex math problems . . .

. . . his finger had a built-in
pencil sharpener . . .

. . . and he could even remove his telescopic eyeball, which made studying the planets much easier.

"Wow," said Ricky. "I can see all the way to Mercury! That's cool!"

CHAPTER 3

Mr. Mosquito Hates Mercury!

Mercury was the smallest planet in the solar system, and it was the closest planet to the sun. But it certainly was not *cool*!

Just ask Mr. Mosquito. He lived on Mercury, and he HATED everything about it!

He hated the long, *long,* HOT days. Each day on Mercury, the temperature rose to more than eight hundred degrees!

Mr. Mosquito couldn't even walk
down the street because his flip-flops
always melted on the sidewalk.

Mr. Mosquito hated Mercury's long, *long,* COLD nights, too. Each night on Mercury, the temperature dropped to almost three hundred degrees below zero!

Mr. Mosquito couldn't
even brush his teeth because
his toothpaste was always
frozen solid!

"I've g-g-got to g-g-get away
f-f-from th-th-this awful p-p-planet,"
said Mr. Mosquito, shivering in the
cold. So Mr. Mosquito looked
through his telescope and saw the
planet Earth.

He saw mice playing happily on
cool autumn days.

He saw them sleeping soundly on
warm summer nights.

"Earth is the planet for me!" said
Mr. Mosquito. "Soon it will be mine!"

CHAPTER 4

Mr. Mosquito Makes His Move

Mr. Mosquito went into his secret laboratory and clipped his filthy fingernails.

He put the clippings into
a giant machine and zapped
them with a powerful ray.

Then, Mr. Mosquito's fingernails
grew and grew and grew . . .

. . . into massive Mutant Mosquitoes!

Mr. Mosquito climbed aboard his spaceship and called to his troops.

"Mutant Mosquitoes," he cried, "it is time to conquer Earth! Follow me!"

And they did.

CHAPTER 5

The Mosquitoes Attack

When Mr. Mosquito got to Earth, he ordered his Mutant Mosquitoes to attack Squeakyville.

Ricky was in math class that afternoon. He looked out the window and saw the Mutant Mosquitoes.

"Uh-oh," said Ricky. "It looks like Squeakyville needs our help!"

Ricky raised his hand.

"May I be excused?" Ricky asked his teacher. "My Robot and I have to save the Earth."

"Not until you've finished your math test," said Ricky's teacher.

Ricky had three problems left. "What is two times three?" he asked himself aloud.

Ricky's Robot was waiting outside. He wanted to help. So he dashed to the teachers' parking lot and brought back some cars.

Ricky's Robot put three cars
into one pile, and he put three
cars into another pile.

Ricky looked at the piles of cars.
"*Two* piles of *three* cars," said
Ricky. "Two times three equals *six*!"

Ricky looked at his next question.
"What is *six* minus *five*?" he asked.
Ricky's Robot knew just what to do.

He threw five of the cars
back into the parking lot.

"I get it," said Ricky. "Six
minus five equals *one*!"

Ricky's last question was the hardest of all.

"What is *one* divided by *two*?" he asked.

The Robot used his mighty karate chop to divide one car in two.

"That was easy," said Ricky. "One divided by two equals *one-half*!"

Ricky handed in his test. Then
he climbed out the window.

"Let's go, Mighty Robot," said
Ricky. "We've got to save the Earth."

"M-m-m-my *car*!" cried Ricky's
teacher.

CHAPTER 6

The Heroes Arrive

Ricky and his Mighty Robot
ran downtown to face the
Mutant Mosquitoes.

The Mosquitoes attacked Ricky's Robot.

"Hey," said Ricky. "Four against one is not fair!"

Then Ricky had an idea.

"Come with me, Robot," said Ricky.

The Mighty Robot was busy fighting, so he could not follow Ricky. But his arm could stretch very far!

Ricky and his Robot's arm stretched all the way to the "Bugs Away" bug-spray factory.

Ricky told the Robot's arm to grab one of the huge bug-spray storage tanks.

Then they headed back to the battle.

CHAPTER 7

A Buggy Battle

The Robot shook the
tank of bug spray.

Then he broke up the buggy
battle with a big blast from
his bionic boot!

CHAPTER 8

Mr. Mosquito's Revenge

The Mutant Mosquitoes had been defeated. Ricky's Mighty Robot chased them into space.

The Mosquitoes flew
back to Mercury and never
bothered anybody again.

Mr. Mosquito was very angry.
He grabbed Ricky and took
him into his spaceship. "Help
me, Robot," Ricky cried.

But it was too late. Mr. Mosquito
chained Ricky up. Then he went
to his control panel and pulled a
secret lever.

Suddenly his spaceship began
to change. It shifted . . .

. . . and grew . . .

. . . and transformed into a giant
Mecha-Mosquito!

The Mecha-Mosquito attacked
Ricky's Mighty Robot. But Ricky's
Robot would not fight back.

He knew that Ricky was inside
the Mecha-Mosquito, and he did
not want his best friend to get hurt.

The Mecha-Mosquito
pounded Ricky's Robot.

What could Ricky do?
Ricky thought and thought.
Then he had an idea.
"Mr. Mosquito," said Ricky,
"I have to go to the bathroom."

"Not now," said Mr. Mosquito.
"I am too busy beating up
your Robot!"

"But it's an emergency," said Ricky.

"Alright, alright," said Mr.
Mosquito. He unlocked Ricky's chains
and led him to the boys' room.

"Hurry up in there!" he yelled.

Inside the bathroom, Ricky
opened a window and stuck
his head outside.

"Pssssst!" Ricky whispered.

The Robot saw Ricky, and
he held out his giant hand.

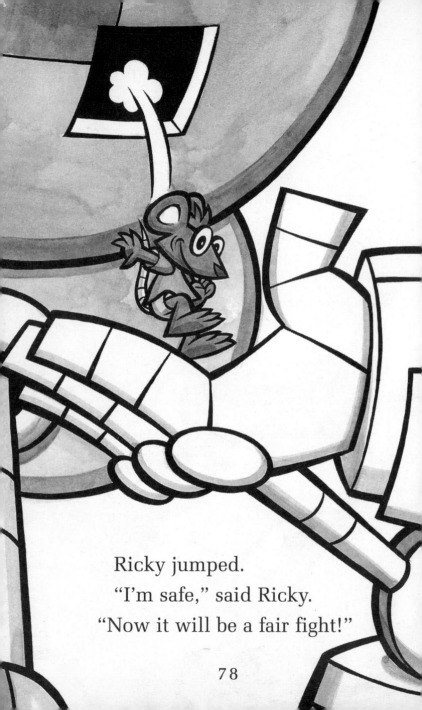

Ricky jumped.
"I'm safe," said Ricky.
"Now it will be a fair fight!"

CHAPTER 9

Ricky's Robot Strikes Back

Inside the Mecha-Mosquito,
Mr. Mosquito was getting very
angry. He knocked on the bathroom
door. "Let's hurry up in there!" he
yelled. "I haven't got all da—"

KER-POW!

Ricky's Robot punched the
Mecha-Mosquito right in the face.

Mr. Mosquito leaped to his
control panel and fought back hard.
The final battle was about to begin.

CHAPTER 10

The Final Battle

(IN FLIP-O-RAMA™)

-RAMA

HERE'S HOW IT WORKS!

STEP 1
Place your *left* hand inside the dotted lines marked "LEFT HAND HERE." Hold the book open *flat*.

STEP 2
Grasp the *right-hand* page with your right thumb and index finger (inside the dotted lines marked "RIGHT THUMB HERE").

STEP 3
Now *quickly* flip the right-hand page back and forth until the picture appears to be *animated*.

(For extra fun, try adding your own sound-effects!)

FLIP-O-RAMA 1

(pages 87 and 89)

Remember, flip *only* page 87.
While you are flipping, be sure
you can see the picture on page 87
and the one on page 89.
If you flip quickly, the two
pictures will start to look like
<u>one</u> *animated* picture.

Don't forget to add
your own sound-effects!

LEFT HAND HERE

The Mecha-Mosquito
Attacked.

87

RIGHT
THUMB
HERE

The Mecha-Mosquito
Attacked.

FLIP-O-RAMA 2

(pages 91 and 93)

Remember, flip *only* page 91.
While you are flipping, be sure
you can see the picture on page 91
and the one on page 93.
If you flip quickly, the two
pictures will start to look like
<u>one</u> *animated* picture.

Don't forget to add
your own sound-effects!

LEFT HAND HERE

Ricky's Robot
Fought Back.

91

RIGHT
THUMB
HERE

Ricky's Robot
Fought Back.

FLIP-O-RAMA 3

(pages 95 and 97)

Remember, flip *only* page 95.
While you are flipping, be sure
you can see the picture on page 95
and the one on page 97.
If you flip quickly, the two
pictures will start to look like
<u>one</u> *animated* picture.

Don't forget to add
your own sound-effects!

LEFT HAND HERE

The Mecha-Mosquito
Battled Hard.

RIGHT
THUMB
HERE

96

The Mecha-Mosquito
Battled Hard.

FLIP-O-RAMA 4

(pages 99 and 101)

Remember, flip *only* page 99.
While you are flipping, be sure
you can see the picture on page 99
and the one on page 101.
If you flip quickly, the two
pictures will start to look like
<u>one</u> *animated* picture.

Don't forget to add
your own sound-effects!

LEFT HAND HERE

Ricky's Robot
Battled Harder.

99

RIGHT
THUMB
HERE

Ricky's Robot
Battled Harder.

FLIP-O-RAMA 5

(pages 103 and 105)

Remember, flip *only* page 103.
While you are flipping, be sure
you can see the picture on page 103
and the one on page 105.
If you flip quickly, the two
pictures will start to look like
<u>one</u> *animated* picture.

Don't forget to add
your own sound-effects!

LEFT HAND HERE

Ricky's Robot
Saved the Day!

RIGHT
THUMB
HERE

Ricky's Robot
Saved the Day!

CHAPTER 11

Justice Prevails

The Mecha-Mosquito
had been destroyed, and
Ricky Ricotta's Mighty
Robot was victorious.

Mr. Mosquito crawled out
of his damaged ship and began
to cry. "What a bad day I am
having," cried Mr. Mosquito.

"It's about to get worse,"
said Ricky.

Ricky's Mighty Robot picked up Mr. Mosquito and dropped him into the Squeakyville jail.

Then Ricky and his Mighty
Robot flew home for chocolate
milk and grilled cheese
sandwiches.

"You boys have saved the world again," said Ricky's mother.

"Yes," said Ricky's father.
"Thank you for sticking together
and fighting for what was right!"
"No problem," said Ricky . . .

... "that's what friends are for."

HOW TO DRAW RICKY

1.

2.

3.

4.

5.

6.

7.

8.

9.

10.

11.

12.

HOW TO DRAW RICKY'S ROBOT

1.

2.

3.

4.

5.

6.

7.

8.

9.

10.

11.

12.

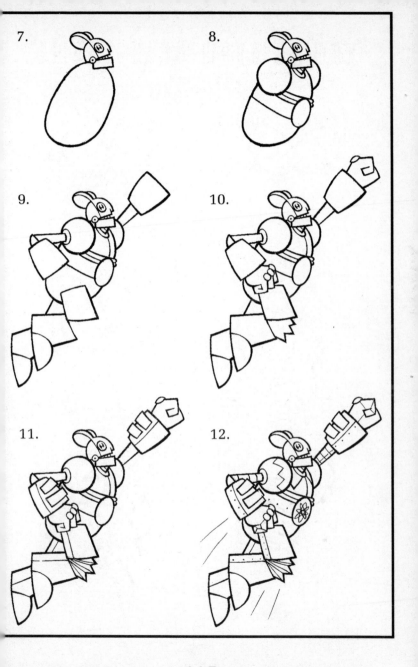

HOW TO DRAW MR. MOSQUITO

1.

2.

3.

4.

5.

6.

118

7.

8.

9.

10.

11.

12.

HOW TO DRAW
A MUTANT MOSQUITO

1.

2.

3.

4.

5.

6.

8.

10.

12.

121

Ricky Ricotta's next adventure
will be to battle
the Voodoo Vultures from Venus!

COMING SOON:

Ricky Ricotta's Mighty Robot

vs.

The Voodoo Vultures from Venus

The Mecha-Monkeys from Mars

The Jurassic Jack Rabbits from Jupiter

The Stupid Stinkbugs from Saturn

The Uranium Unicorns from Uranus

The Naughty Night Crawlers from Neptune

The Un-Pleasant Penguins from Pluto

About the Author and Illustrator

DAV PILKEY created his first stories as comic books while he was in elementary school. In 1997, he wrote and illustrated his first adventure novel for children, *The Adventures of Captain Underpants*, which received rave reviews and was an instant bestseller—as were the three books that followed in the series. Dav is also the creator of numerous award-winning picture books, including *The Paperboy*, a Caldecott Honor Book, and the Dumb Bunnies books. He and his dog live in Portland, Oregon.

It was a stroke of luck when Dav discovered the work of artist **MARTIN ONTIVEROS**. Dav knew that Martin was just the right illustrator for the Ricky Ricotta's Mighty Robot series. Martin also lives in Portland, Oregon. He has a lot of toys as well as two cats, Bunny and Spanky.